WORLD DISASTERS!

EARTHQUAKE

BRIAN KNAPP

STECK-VAUGHN
L I B R A R Y

Austin, Texas

Published in the United States in 1990 by Steck-Vaughn Co., Austin, Texas, a subsidiary of National Education Corporation

First published in 1989
by Macmillan Children's Books
A division of Macmillan Publishers Ltd

Designed and produced by Earthscape Editions, Sonning Common, Oxon, England

Cover design by Julian Holland

Illustrations by
Duncan McCrae and Tim Smith

Printed and bound in the United States.

2 3 4 5 6 7 8 9 0 LB 95 94 93 92 91 90

Library of Congress Cataloging-in-Publication Data

Knapp, Brian J.
    Earthquake

    (World disasters!)
    "First published in 1989 by Macmillan Children's Books"—T.p. verso.
    Summary: Describes the natural phenomena that cause earthquakes, landslides, and tsunamis. Discusses why people die in such catastrophes and what they can do to protect themselves and their property.
    1. Earthquakes—Juvenile literature.   [1. Earthquakes]
I. McCrae, Duncan, Ill.   II. Smith, Tim, ill.   III. Title.
IV. Series: Knapp, Brian J. World Disasters!
QE521.3.K52   1990
363.3′495   89-21574
ISBN 0-8114-2375-1

Acknowledgments

The publishers wish to thank William Milian in Mexico City for his invaluable assistance in the preparation of this book.

Photographic credits

t = top b = bottom l-left r = right

All photographs are from the Earthscape Editions photographic library except for the following title page, 12, 20b Colorific; contents page 7, 17, 24, 27, 28b, 29, 39b, USGS; 37t British Museum (Natural History); 26, 32, 34b, 35 A. Gonzalez/Reflex; 28t Frank Lane Picture Agency; 10t, 10b, 11t, 11b, 13t, 13b, 34t W. Milian, 30 30 Popperfoto, 161, 16b ZEFA.

Cover: Rex Features Ltd
Earthquake damage in Mexico City

Note to the reader
In this book there are some words in the text that are printed in **bold** type. This shows that the word is listed in the glossary on page 46. The glossary gives a brief explanation of words that may be new to you.

Contents

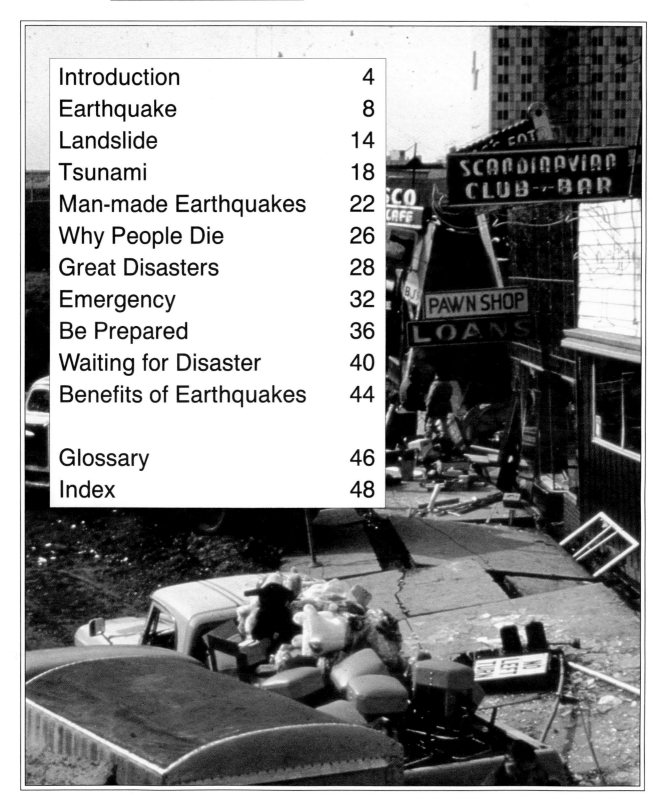

Introduction	4
Earthquake	8
Landslide	14
Tsunami	18
Man-made Earthquakes	22
Why People Die	26
Great Disasters	28
Emergency	32
Be Prepared	36
Waiting for Disaster	40
Benefits of Earthquakes	44
Glossary	46
Index	48

Introduction

An **earthquake** usually begins deep within the Earth. When one strikes, the surface of the ground shakes violently. Earthquakes can cause **disaster** when they result in human injury and death.

Why do earthquake disasters happen? To understand this, we must first find out something about the part played by earthquakes in the history of the Earth.

Inside the Earth

The Earth is made up of many different materials. The outer zone is the solid rock called the **crust,** which is fashioned into continents and oceans, mountains and valleys. It forms the land on which we live and the land underneath the oceans. Beneath the crust is another zone of material called the **mantle,** and inside this lies the **core.** These zones of rock are in layers somewhat like the layers of an onion.

All Earth's rocks contain **radioactive** materials which release heat, just as they do in a nuclear power station. There is such intense heat and pressure within the Earth that some of the inner zones have melted and become fire-hot liquids. The top part of the mantle has become partly liquid, which means that the crust, which is our home, now floats on top, just like a log floating on a pond.

In the mantle, the molten rock is continually moving, just as water does when it is heated and boils in a saucepan.

This movement is called **convection.** In some regions, the rock moves apart, and in others it moves together. As the mantle rock moves, it drags the brittle crust with it, causing great splits to open up. At the present time the crust is broken into over a dozen large pieces, each one called a crustal **plate.** The splitting has broken the Earth's surface much like a giant eggshell that has just been cracked with a spoon.

The relatively thin crustal plates are dragged in many directions. In some places they are pulled apart, and in others crushed together. Sometimes plates are dragged past one another. However, no matter what is happening to the crustal plates, it is at the boundaries between one and another that earthquakes usually happen.

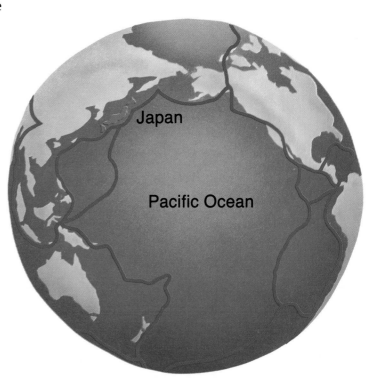

_____ plate edges

▶ *The Earth's crust has been split into more than a dozen large plates. Notice that the edges of the plates do not necessarily match the edges of the continents. This view of the Earth shows that the largest plate forms much of the Pacific Ocean.*

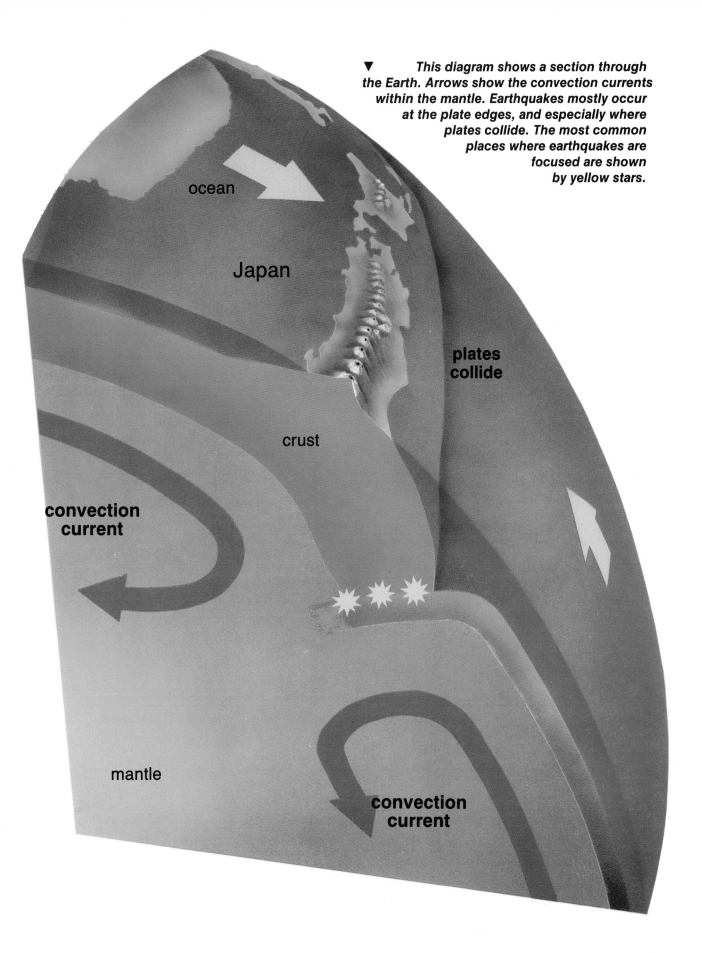

▼ This diagram shows a section through the Earth. Arrows show the convection currents within the mantle. Earthquakes mostly occur at the plate edges, and especially where plates collide. The most common places where earthquakes are focused are shown by yellow stars.

ocean

Japan

plates collide

crust

convection current

convection current

mantle

Risk of disaster

Because earthquakes occur mostly at plate boundaries, people in the center of continents have less to worry about. Where plates are pulling apart earthquakes are common but usually very minor. The main risk lies where plates are either crushing together or slipping past one another.

Places that are not near plate boundaries, however, sometimes still experience earthquakes for a rather strange reason. Rocks have a "long memory." They may have been put under pressure hundreds of millions of years ago but they still have that pressure locked into them. While the pressure is held in check, usually by the weight of rocks piled on top, they will remain still. However, if the balance should change, the pressure will then be released and there will be an earthquake. One of the world's most powerful earthquakes, at New Madrid, Missouri, was of this type (p. 29). So no one can really count on being safe from earthquakes.

Types of earthquake effect

Earthquakes usually begin deep within the crust when the pressure between parts of the crustal plates has built up too much for them to be held in place. Then the ground snaps and sends **shock waves** out in all directions. The place where the earthquake begins is called the **focus.** The land immediately above the focus however, may not be the place where the most damage occurs. The amount of the damage depends on the size of the shock waves and what kind of ground is being shaken. An earthquake that is only strong enough to shake hard rock a little, may be able to make weak materials shake very strongly indeed. This is what happened in Mexico City (p. 9).

▼ *The main earthquake zones, and the places of greatest risk, are concentrated along the edges of the crustal plates. The places where plates collide have the largest number of major earthquakes.*

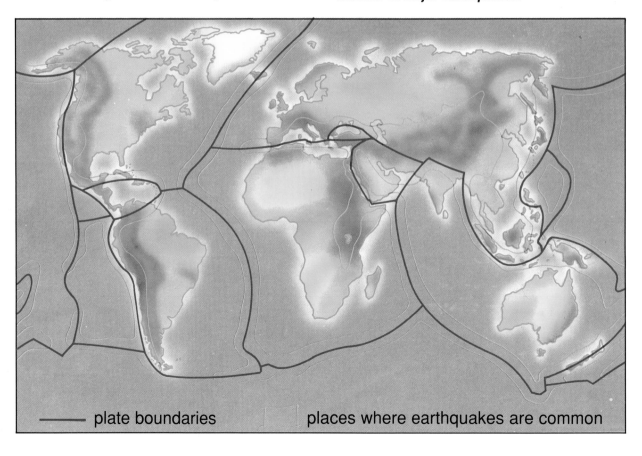

—— plate boundaries　　　□ places where earthquakes are common

▶ *Earthquakes are associated with three types of fault, one of which can be seen in this landscape. The most common type of fault occurs when one slab of rock falls vertically against another. This is called a normal fault. If a slab is pushed vertically upward, it gives a reversed fault. Where plates slide past one another without any significant vertical movement, it is called a thrust fault. The San Andreas thrust fault in California, is shown in this picture.*

Earthquakes do much more than just shake the ground. In some places the ground splits apart, along a line called a **fault.** In other places, where there is loose rock and soil, ground vibrations can start landslides. Some water-filled soils can behave like quicksand when they are shaken, losing all their strength, so that buildings sink into them. Lastly, an earthquake under the ocean often sets up waves in the sea which come ashore as giant waves called **tsunami.** Each one of these effects, by itself, has killed large numbers of people in the past.

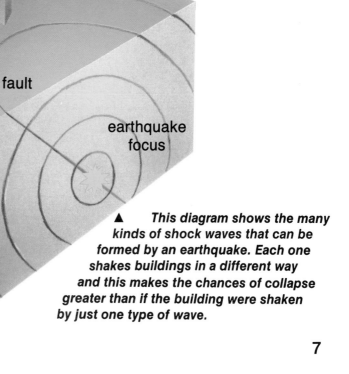

city

fault

earthquake
focus

shock waves

▲ *This diagram shows the many kinds of shock waves that can be formed by an earthquake. Each one shakes buildings in a different way and this makes the chances of collapse greater than if the building were shaken by just one type of wave.*

Earthquake

Earthquakes are happening all the time, and they usually last for a few minutes. Each year about 800,000 quakes (called **tremors**) are recorded, but most of these are too small to be noticed. A big earthquake, causing widespread damage, can be expected somewhere in the world every 50 to 100 years. During the time between tremors strain builds up gradually in the rocks. Then, when the earthquake occurs, all the stored energy is released in a few minutes. It is like pulling back the string of a bow very slowly and then releasing it suddenly to fire an arrow.

The power of an earthquake

The amount of energy released when the rocks snap and an earthquake strikes is about the same as a firework going off for each cubic yard of rock moved. That doesn't sound like much—but a great deal of rock is moved during a quake. Often rock slips along a line about 60 miles in length and about 60 miles deep, and rock over 30 miles away, on either side of the fault line may be moved. The amount of energy needed to cause this movement is enormous. This energy is equal to setting off a thousand one-megaton (one million ton) nuclear bombs—enough to destroy every single person on Earth.

▶ *The focus of the Mexico City earthquake was many hundreds of miles to the west of the city. However, Mexico City is built on soft muds which were easily shaken when the shock waves reached them. Nearby places on strong, hard rock were not affected as badly.*

The Mexico City disaster

An earthquake is one of the most terrifying experiences that people can suffer. They come without warning and no one can make any preparations. In some parts of the world people just have to learn to live with the threat that one morning they may wake to find the world collapsing around them. This is exactly what happened in 1985 in Mexico City, which is built on wet mud and swampland. When this land was hit by the shock waves it shook just like a giant bowl of jelly, destroying many buildings and killing thousands of people.

A small newsboy named Pedro lived through that earthquake, and still remembers what it was like.

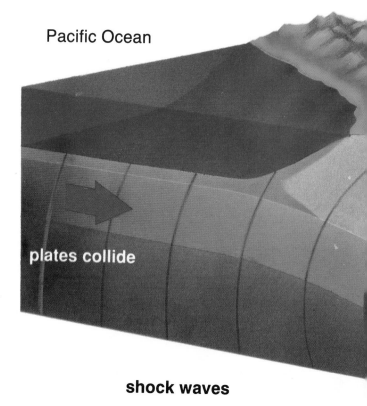

Pacific Ocean

plates collide

shock waves

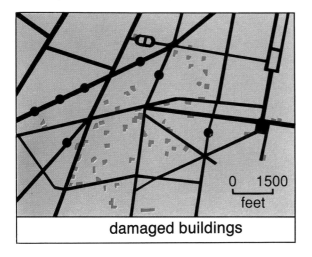

▼ *This map of the center of Mexico City shows the large number of buildings that were destroyed. The large number of office buildings demolished—and the loss of vital paperwork that they contained, made sorting out the future of the city that much harder.*

damaged buildings

The shaking

It started early in the morning. The vast army of people that work in the center of Mexico City each day were crowding onto buses, sitting in their private cars at a standstill along with the other traffic, or being squashed like sardines in the subways. Pedro was selling newspapers to the commuters as they waited at the traffic lights of a busy intersection. At 7:18 it was just an ordinary day. At 7:19 something strange and terrifying began to happen. The ground beneath Pedro's feet began to tremble. He steadied himself. The trembling went away and he went on trying to sell his newspapers. Then the whole ground began to shake so violently that he could no longer stay on his feet. The asphalt began heaving up and down, bouncing cars around. People were screaming and shouting. Pedro caught sight of the giant Pemex Tower: its 50 floors were shaking back and forth!

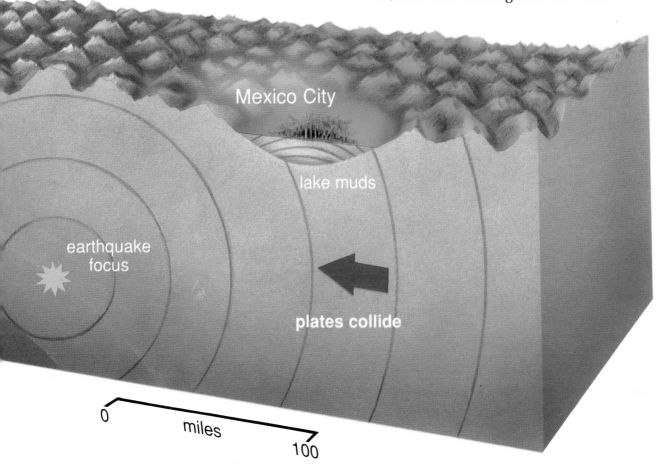

Buildings collapse

A nearby office building in the street began to come apart with a dreadful wrenching sound. A piece of the wall fell away and Pedro could see the office furniture inside shaking up and down. Then the corner of the building began to twist, sliding as though in slow motion before it crashed to the ground.

People on the pavement were crushed under the falling building. A second later another office building folded up. The walls gave way and the roof fell onto the floor below. Unable to support this extra weight the floor fell through. Then each floor crushed the floor below, including any people who were inside. Within seconds a ten-story building was changed into a pile of giant slabs stacked one on top of the other. Pedro could do nothing. He couldn't help other people and he couldn't help himself. He lay on the ground crying while the earth continued to shake beneath him. More walls and whole buildings crashed to the ground as though they had been hit by a bomb.

▲ ▼ *These two photographs show what the central area of Mexico City looked like before the earthquake and soon afterward. Only the giant Pemex building remains unscathed.*

10

While the earthquake lasted only a few minutes, it managed to transform the center of Mexico City into a scene of utter destruction. It left thousands dead and many more thousands trapped in the heaps of rubble.

The earthquake ends

As soon as the tremors stopped people began hunting for their relatives and friends who were trapped, perhaps injured or killed, in the buildings that had collapsed. Pedro thought of his parents in the suburbs— were they all right? How could he find out with no buses moving on the cracked and rubble-littered roads? After a moment he began walking home, so stunned that he could hardly think straight. In his mind he already knew that thousands must be dead.

◄   *Walls fell away from the office building exposing the floors inside. Fortunately the whole building did not collapse.*

▼   *Little remains of the building. Each floor collapsed on the one underneath.*

▶ *Rescue parties scramble over the wreckage of a collapsed building, using their bare hands to search for any survivors.*

The rescue

Pedro's story shows what an earthquake is like. When one is happening, the forces of nature are so powerful that people can do nothing but try to save their own lives. Even when it is over, many dangers and problems still need to be overcome.

The biggest worry in Mexico City was that gas might have escaped from the broken fuel and gas pipes. Sparks from broken electricity cables could easily have started an explosion or set off a raging fire.

When some buildings did catch fire, firefighters could only stand and watch because the water pipes had broken.

Rubble from the fallen buildings was lying all over the street and abandoned and crushed cars littered the streets. It was almost impossible for help to get to the scene quickly because many roads were blocked. There was a great shortage of cranes and bulldozers to clear the streets and allow desperately needed ambulances to get through. In some cases this took days. Buildings that had not collapsed were

▼ *Crowbars were the most effective means of turning over the rubble in the search for buried people. Until all the injured had been brought out, heavy lifting gear could not be used.*

dangerous and had to be shored up before rescue teams could go in. Hospitals were damaged and could not cope with the huge numbers of injured people. Tens of thousands were homeless.

In the long term

When all these immediate problems had been dealt with, others began to appear. For example, because there was no clean water for days, the risk of disease was high. One of the priorities therefore became the vaccination of all those in the destruction zone.

▶ *Rescue teams had to proceed with immense care because many people were trapped between floors that were in danger of collapse. This boy was rescued from his bedroom more than a day after the earthquake.*

The main area of destruction was confined to the city center because, although there are more than 20 million people in the city, most of them live in small shacks in the slums. The poorly built shacks, with their walls made of poles and old scraps of sheet steel are fortunately very resistant to earthquake damage. However, houses made from mud and sticks cracked and collapsed.

Over the next few years money will have to be found to rebuild the city—and Mexico is a poor country. A few of the office buildings were sufficiently insured so that their owners could rebuild them, but many were not. The government simply does not have the money to help either the offices or those in the slums. Here people will have to rebuild for themselves. As a result of all these problems, Mexico City is likely to remain scarred by the earthquake for many years to come.

Landslide

▼ The location of Yungay in the Andes.

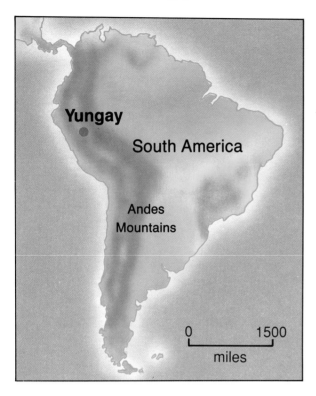

Yungay

South America

Andes
Mountains

0   1500
miles

Nothing can withstand a violent earthquake. In mountainous areas blocks of rock are shaken free, plunging down slopes to valleys below. On slopes covered with soil the whole valley side can vibrate, releasing great slabs of soil and rock or shaking soil into a powder. Neither steep nor gentle slopes can be considered safe in an earthquake.

The fate of Yungay

When rocks break free from steep mountain slopes, they often bounce to the valley floor without causing much damage, because not many people live in these mountain areas. **Landslides** can sometimes be of enormous proportions and by a quirk of bad luck can sometimes occur above towns in the bottom of a valley. This disastrous combination happened one awful day in Peru.

Peru is a South American country straddling the Andes. Some of the highest mountains in the world are found in the Andes and from these high spots, glaciers have flowed to the ocean, gouging deep, steep-sided, and narrow valleys on their way. The only place that soil builds up and grass and crops can grow is on the floors of these valleys. People huddle into towns that are usually located where valleys meet. One such town was called Yungay.

In 1970 the shock waves from an earthquake in the Andes shook the whole mountain area near Yungay, and caused the deaths of 20,000 people. The event that created the devastation happened high up on one of the mountains called Huascaran. Here a huge mass of glacier ice was balanced above the valley side, resting on rock that had been cracked loose by many years of frost action. When the earthquake struck, both the ice and the rock rubble fell over a high precipice and cascaded to the valley below. This mass was absolutely enormous. It contained over 60 million cubic yards of material.

As the rock and ice crashed down to the valley floor the ice melted and the material changed into a rock-filled **mudflow**.

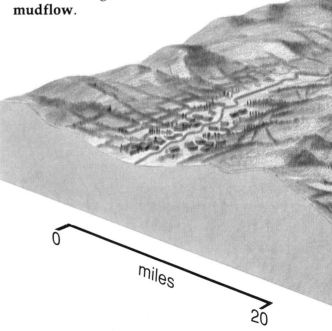

0

miles

20

The mudflow reached a speed faster than any racing car. Within minutes it had increased to over 250 miles an hour. This superfast flow tore down the valley, gathering more water and rock as it went. It was like a huge unstoppable battering ram. In its path lay the town of Yungay with its 22,000 inhabitants.

The mudflow made a deep rumbling sound, and some people heard it coming. A few realized they were in danger and tried to scramble to a little hill that formed the core of the town. They had just three minutes to make it and they were the only ones to survive. When the mudflow hit Yungay it wiped the town off the map. It carried away buildings and buried the ruins in mud. Over 20,000 people were killed instantly.

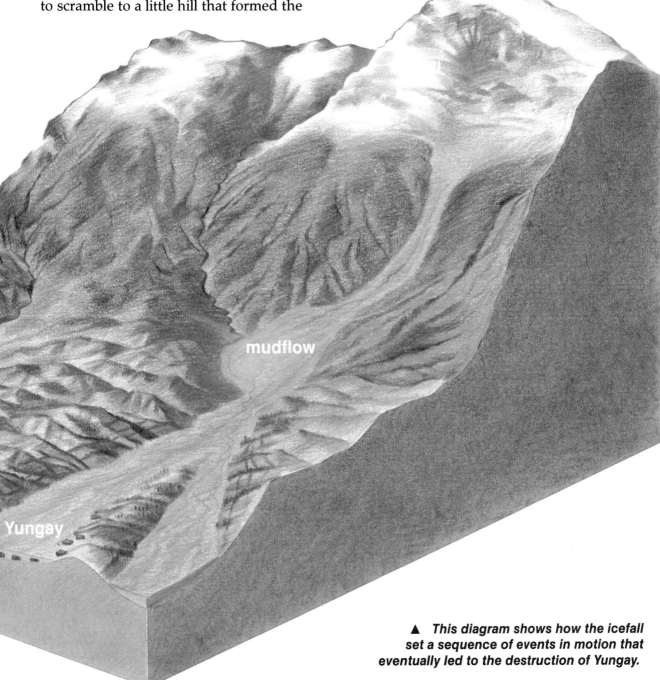

Mount Huascaran

mudflow

Yungay

▲ *This diagram shows how the icefall set a sequence of events in motion that eventually led to the destruction of Yungay.*

▶ *This photograph shows the view toward Huascaran before the mudflow. The mountain and its glacier ice seem to be very far away. The ice fell from the left hand peak.*

▼ *After the earthquake caused the mudflow Yungay was completely buried or carried away by the mudflow. The great scar created by the icefall shows clearly on the left hand peak. Below it is a brown trail that marks the start of the region of destruction.*

◄ *Only the remains of the monastery and this statue of Christ survived to mark the spot where the center of Yungay used to be. The remains of a building can be seen in the foreground, buried under the cobblestones carried along by the mudflow.*

Disaster for Vaiont

Vaiont was a small town set high in the Italian Alps, and, like Yungay, it was in the bottom of a deep mountain valley. A few years before, a large dam had been built across the valley just upstream of the town. It was one of the world's tallest dams and the water held back behind it was over 300 feet deep.

Some people had noticed many of the rocks on the slopes of the valley had gaping fissures in them. They said that this meant that new landslides would soon happen. But no one listened to them.

All went well in Vaiont until the earthquake struck on October 9, 1963. It was not a large earthquake like the one in the Andes, but it was enough. A huge piece of the mountain—about 260 million cubic yards in volume—broke free and fell into the water. The splash it made sent a wave 300 feet high over the crest of the dam. As the water hit the valley floor below it smashed the town of Vaiont apart and the 2,000 people who lived there were drowned.

▶ *This map shows the locality of the silt hills of China where landslides occur.*

Landslides in China

Large areas of China have low hills made of a loose **silty** soil that is very fertile. It is rich land for farming. This good farmland, however, is also very fragile because China suffers many large earthquakes. When a tremor is felt, the silty hills vibrate, turning into a kind of quicksand. Soil from the hills flows down into the valleys and buries people, making the hills very dangerous places to be.

In the famous T'ang-shan region in 1556 an earthquake dislodged vast amounts of this silt. About 830,000 people were killed. The exact number isn't known because records kept at the time are not accurate. Still, it was the largest earthquake disaster known in human history.

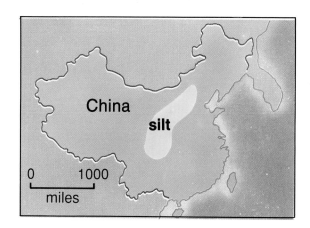

China
silt

0   1000
miles

Tsunami

Earthquake disasters don't just take place in the area near the focus. In some cases many lives are lost far away. For example, many thousands may be killed and their homes destroyed when they are hit by a giant sea wave called a tsunami.

How a tsunami strikes

Tsunami is a Japanese word describing one of the most terrifying natural events in the world—a huge water wave that rushes onto shore following an earthquake.

Out at sea tsunami waves look quite harmless. Here the killer waves may be less than three feet high. But they can be up to 60 miles broad (from crest to crest) and many hundreds of miles wide. This means that, although it is barely noticeable to ships out in the ocean, an enormous amount of water is on the move in a tsunami as it starts to travel.

Tsunamis can also move at terrific speed—as much as 375 miles an hour—the same speed as a modern jet plane. Out in the deep areas of the Pacific Ocean, however, no one notices this speed, because the waves never grow too much more than a few inches in height.

When tsunamis reach the shallow water near a coast they change dramatically. The shallow water slows down the wave,

small wave height in deep ocean

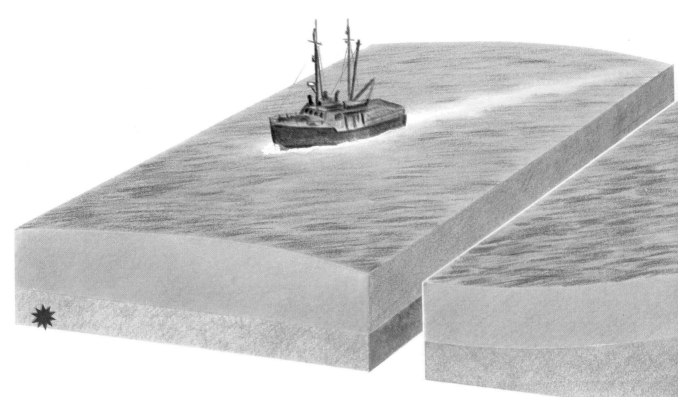

▲ *An earthquake causes the sea bed to shake, setting a giant wave in motion. Notice how the wave is low and wide as it travels over the deep ocean, but that it rears up dramatically on reaching the shallow water at the coast.*

but the water following behind still keeps moving forward. So a huge amount of moving water piles up on the shore. By this means, tsunamis can become incredible towering giants sometimes over 80 feet high within seconds. These waves surge onto the land washing people and houses away as they go.

The cause of tsunamis

When a pebble is thrown inland into the still waters of a pond, there is a "plop" and then the pebble disappears. But at the place where it entered the water a train of ripples spreads out silently, eventually lapping against the nearby shore. If an earthquake happens beneath an ocean, the ocean bed shakes and sets up waves just as if a giant pebble had been thrown into the water. The waves then spread out in all directions until they reach some far-off coast.

A tsunami is made up of a number of waves just like those that come from the pebble in the pond. As each wave arrives it causes destruction and flooding, sometimes as far as one mile from the shore. Then, when the energy is spent, the water rushes back out to sea, scouring the land as it goes. A few minutes later, the next wave hits and the pattern of destruction begins all over again.

wave rears up on reaching coast

coastal villages and towns submerged by surging wave.

◀ ▼ *The upper picture shows people sunbathing on a beach. The lower picture shows how, in 1964 a similar peaceful coastline in Alaska was transformed into a scene of destruction by a tsunami. Large fishing boats were carried onshore by the surging wave, while cars and even houses were picked up and smashed.*

There is no warning from a tsunami—no bad weather or strong winds to hint of possible danger. Because the earthquake happens so far away, no ground shocks are felt either. The wave approaches at the speed of an express train and people have no chance to run for safety. Within seconds they are caught up in the huge wave, tossed about along with houses, trees, and any other debris in its path. There is little chance of escape.

Where do tsunamis strike?

Tsunamis need special conditions to grow. They must be formed in deep oceans because they need a large space to develop in. And they must be produced by earthquakes. The Pacific Ocean is large and deep, and it is surrounded by the "**Pacific Ring of Fire**," a ring of crustal plate edges where a great many earthquakes occur. This is the main breeding ground for tsunamis.

About 90 percent of all recorded tsunamis take place in the Pacific Ocean. Islands like the Hawaiian Islands, in the middle of the Pacific, are particularly at risk. Since 1819 over 100 tsunamis have hit the shores of Hawaii. Tsunamis have also destroyed coastal settlements in Alaska and swept across the coast of California. It is Japan, however, where most lives have been lost. Waves over 65 feet high drowned 27,000 Japanese in 1896. Not many tsunamis strike in the Atlantic Ocean, but in 1755 an earthquake struck off the coast of Portugal. Tsunami waves were probably responsible for many of the 60,000 deaths that resulted.

Coasts of greatest risk

In some places the risk of destruction is greater than in others. The risk is greatest on volcanic islands like Hawaii, where the ocean bed rises swiftly from the deep ocean. A deep ocean allows tsunami waves to travel quickly without losing much of their power. This means that the land has to absorb the full force of the tsunami wave and it will do a lot of damage. By contrast, a tsunami, reaching a coast where the ocean floor shelves gently, loses much of its force as it brushes against the sand and rock.

Because of this factor, there is a great variation in the risk at different places along the coast of Hawaii. The zones with the lowest risk from a large tsunami wave (marked yellow on the map below) are places where the ocean floor is relatively gentle and much of the energy of the tsunami wave will be absorbed before it reaches the land. However, the purple zones show where the ocean floor is steepest and the risk of being struck by a large wave is therefore very high.

▼ *This map of Hawaii in the Pacific Ocean, shows how the tsunami hazard varies around the coast. Places in hazard zone 2 can expect tsunamis with wave heights up to 15 feet; in zone 3 wave heights may reach 30 feet; in zone 4 waves could be up to 50 feet high; in zone 5 they may reach more than 50 feet.*

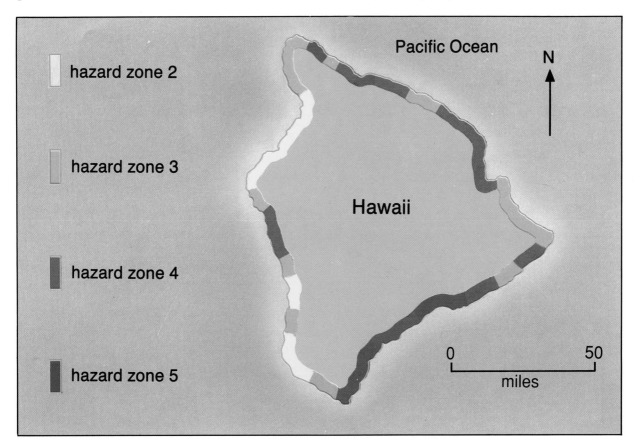

hazard zone 2

hazard zone 3

hazard zone 4

hazard zone 5

Pacific Ocean

N

Hawaii

0   50
miles

Man-made Earthquakes

A large earthquake can have energy equal to a thousand megaton nuclear bomb; and it starts many hundreds of miles below the surface of the Earth. So how could people possibly turn an earthquake on and off? The idea may seem stupid, but experience has shown that it can happen. People do not have to apply enough pressure directly to snap a rock, they only have to unbalance the natural forces. Some rocks can be very finely balanced between remaining firm or snapping. In areas that have suffered from many earthquakes in the past, the rocks may need only a small change before they, too, snap and start a tremor.

Hoover's near miss

The possibility of altering the balance was first discovered by accident when the giant Hoover Dam, between Nevada and Arizona, was being filled for the first time. The Hoover Dam was built in the 1930s to hold back the waters of the Colorado River and create a large lake, called Lake Mead. The lake was to be used to irrigate several states and bring life to the nearby desert.

The dam is one of the world's tallest, its huge curved wall blocking a canyon near Las Vegas. When the dam was finished and the water began to fill the lake, people found that something very strange was happening. As the water got higher and higher, earthquakes began to happen. They became more and more frequent and more and more violent.

▶ *The Hoover Dam is over 320 feet high. Its huge curved wall holds back a lake over 90 miles long.*

With the lake nearly full the engineers began to wonder if the earthquakes would crack the dam. The largest quake registered 5.0 on the **Richter scale** and occurred soon after the lake reached its highest level in 1939. Fortunately, the dam held firm. Gradually, with the water held at a steady level, the number and size of earthquakes decreased. Today there are few quakes and they are so small the millions of people who cross the dam each year never notice them.

The Hoover Dam was one of the first really large dams. No one had suspected that the filling of a **reservoir** could have these side effects. But as more and more tall dams were built it became clear that earthquakes always occurred as the reservoirs were filled. So engineers were able to turn earthquakes on, although they could not control their size and effect.

▼ **This chart shows the number of earthquakes that occurred as the Hoover Dam was closed and the reservoir was filled. Notice that the number of earthquakes was dramatically reduced as soon as the water level became steady.**

Engineers now fill the reservoirs much more slowly. This gives a chance for the rocks to adjust to the weight of the water without setting off big earthquakes.

▼ **The area downstream from the Hoover Dam contains many settlements. If the dam had failed due to earthquake damage many people would have been killed.**

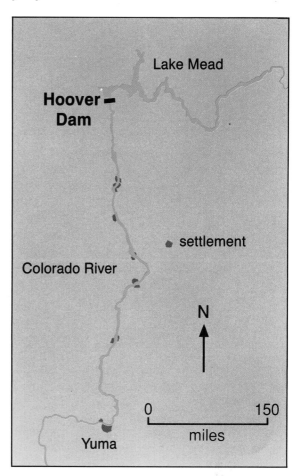

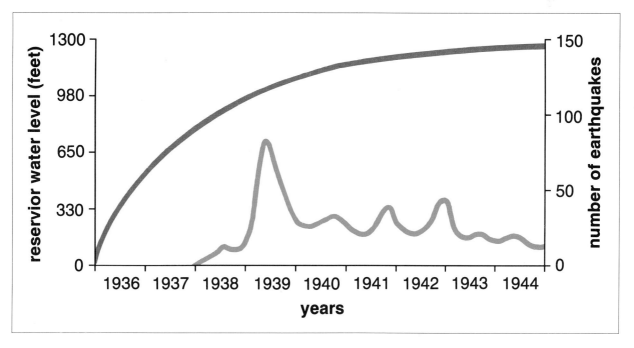

Dam disaster in India

In India a man-made earthquake caused a disaster at the Koyna Dam in 1967. The engineers expected some quakes as they filled the reservoir, but an earthquake occurred right under the center of the dam's wall. The wall cracked, and the force of the earthquake (6.3 on the Richter scale) killed 200 people, injured 1,500 more, and left thousands homeless.

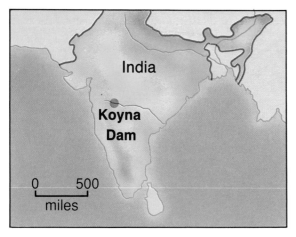

A chance to control quakes?

Some people believe that one day we might be able to control earthquakes by using an effect discovered in deep oil wells.

To increase the flow of oil from fields that are nearly exhausted, water is often pumped down other wells within the oil field to try to push the remaining oil out. However, whenever water is forced down wells, it starts up small earthquakes in some areas. Geologists discovered that since the rocks are all under pressure, the effect of the pumped-in water is to unlock old faults, causing the rocks to slip and producing earthquakes.

◄   *The location of the Koyna Dam, India.*

▼   *This photograph shows part of a hospital in California that collapsed during an earthquake in 1971.*

▶ *A map of California shows that the state is criss-crossed with faults. Each line shows where earthquakes have moved the crust in the past. Most of the faults are still active. Any plan to control the quakes would have to be applied to all of these faults. It would be a mammoth task.*

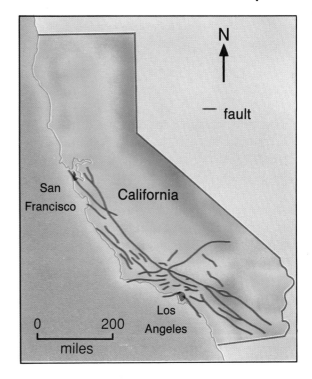

Based on these findings some people had the idea that the dangerous energy building up in faults in California could be released little by little by pumping water into the faults. If this could be done then the disastrous earthquake that San Francisco has been expecting might be avoided.

Great earthquakes, however, usually release far more energy than all the small ones combined. So the only way to prevent a major earthquake would be to cause large earthquakes anyway. It would probably not be possible to cause enough unnoticeable quakes to release the locked-up energy. And no one would be prepared to accept the damage that would be caused by setting off large quakes.

◀ *The caption to this cartoon reads "On second thought. I think I'd rather wait for the real thing."*

This type of cartoon tells us that many people are worried by tests to control earthquakes. They fear that the tests will cause as much damage as a real earthquake, but that they will occur much more often.

Why People Die

There is nothing to show when an earthquake is about to happen—nothing to remind or warn people. Heavy clouds in the sky or massive volcanic mountains nearby both remind people of possible disaster. However, an earthquake is different. It is invisible, it comes without warning, and it comes quickly. This is one reason so many people die.

Collapsing buildings

The earthquake that devastated parts of Guatemala shows why so many die. Guatemala is in Central America, and it is a hilly country with many steep slopes. People live at the tops of steep slopes or in valleys at the foot of the slopes. When an earthquake begins, there are often massive landslides. Now there are only big scars to show that land slipped into the valleys in 1976 and buried thousands of people.

The earthquake came at 3:02 a.m., and lasted only 30 seconds. There was no time to react. Everyone was in bed asleep. Had it been during the day people would have been outdoors working in the fields and fewer lives might have been lost. In the 300 villages that were damaged, most people died as their brick houses collapsed on top of them before they could get out of bed.

The final death toll was 23,000, with 77,000 more injured and over one million left homeless. A fifth of the country's entire population suffered as a result of this short earthquake.

▼　*People died in this building because it had not been designed to withstand shocks. When the earthquake struck it collapsed like a pack of cards.*

► *These buildings were constructed on a steep slope liable to experience landslides. A survey of the ground before construction would have shown it as an unsafe place to build.*

Unprepared

Were there any precautions people could have taken? To start with, they could have used different materials for their houses, instead of bricks and mortar and heavy tiles on their roofs. In an earthquake, mortar cracks and walls collapse. When heavy tiles fall they crush people.

People die because they do not change their building methods. As soon as the earthquake in Guatemala was over people were looking for enough bricks in the rubble to build their homes again—just the same way as before.

The tsunami threat

Earthquakes come without warning, although the areas of high risk are known. The sea waves called tsunamis also arrive without warning. They bring death to people far from an earthquake zone and often thousands of miles from the earthquake focus.

Tsunamis can be predicted. Yet people still die. One reason is lack of warning. It is easy to warn people by radio and television in a country like the United States, but people in poor countries don't always have radios and televisions. The villages where they live usually don't have telephones.

Tsunamis can travel at hundreds of miles an hour, and if a warning is not given within an hour of the quake, it may be too late.

Ignoring warnings

Warnings will save lives. The trouble is that they often go unheeded.

In Crescent City, California, the people were warned that there might be a tsunami after an earthquake had struck in Alaska. The Civil Defense evacuated people from the part of the coast in danger, and when the first two waves hit there was little risk to life. However, then the townspeople made up their minds that the worst was over and they could return home in spite of advice to the contrary. No sooner had they done so when the next wave struck—an even bigger wave than the first two. Many people were trapped in their homes and killed.

Warnings that can cause death

Warnings can also backfire. When the people of San Francisco heard of the tsunami warning in 1964, ten thousand people flocked to the coast to see it arrive. They treated it as a tourist attraction. They didn't realize how big a tsunami could be— and they certainly didn't realize it could cause deaths.

Great Disasters

There are no signs saying that an earthquake is on the way, and no way to tell how severe it will be. Sometimes an earthquake will just make the ground tremble and plates shake on a shelf, but at other times it can bring death or ruin. In China, in 1976, about 700,000 people were killed as the result of one earthquake.

Sometimes the worst effects of a disaster are avoided. In 1964, for example, the people of Anchorage, Alaska, were enjoying the end of a fine sunny Good Friday. Since it was a public holiday, the shops, schools, and offices were closed. Nearly everybody was out in the country or sailing on the water. At 5:36 p.m. a large

▼ *The main street in Anchorage, Alaska, soon after the earthquake. It was a major disaster because it caused enormous damage to the economy of the state.*

▼ *A complete section of Anchorage's main street dropped several yards. The vehicles in the foreground were left below the road surface and the shop behind them had its ground floor turned into a basement.*

earthquake struck. Buildings collapsed and there was a great deal of damage, but only 114 people were killed. That figure would have been much greater if everyone had been indoors. Imagine what the death toll might have been if the quake had struck at 11 a.m. on a winter's day.

Some major disasters

We can't be certain just how many people have been killed by earthquakes since humans have lived on the Earth, but scientists think the number may be as great as 100 million. This century on average, over 15,000 people have died in earthquakes each year, and in some individual years the death toll is tremendous.

The biggest earthquake

What was the biggest earthquake that ever happened? Although no one really knows, the quake of 1812 in New Madrid, Missouri, must have been close to the all-time record. The shock waves even rang church bells in Washington, D.C., a thousand miles away! It was also the least expected, because as far as anyone knew, there had never been an earthquake anywhere near there before.

It was Christmastime, and everyone was looking forward to the festivities when the first quake happened on December 16, 1811. A series of quakes followed that continued until February 1812. Shock after shock went through the town, some so

▲ *Much of San Francisco was destroyed by the earthquake of 1906. All of the houses that used to stand in the foreground of this picture have been leveled and the curbstone buckled by the force of the quake.*

severe that they were felt right across America, from the Gulf Coast to the Canadian border, from the Atlantic seaboard to the Rockies. At the end, New Madrid's wooden houses were no more than matchwood; its inhabitants had experienced the largest earthquake ever recorded in North America. Even the course of the great Mississippi River was changed in several places as a new landscape was produced.

The most famous disaster

San Francisco is a city built on several hills overlooking the ocean and a bay. It is a spectacular place. If people had learned from the earthquakes of 1838 and 1865 they would have stopped building and gone elsewhere, for underneath the city lies one of the world's great earthquake zones.

▲ *San Francisco's city hall was left in ruins by the earthquake of 1906. Notice that the main tower of the building stands because it contained a steel frame.*

However, by 1906 buildings were going up more quickly than ever. On April 18th an earthquake measuring 8.2 on the Richter scale rocked the city just after 5 a.m. It destroyed buildings for 30 miles on either side of the earthquake center.

The main shock lasted about a minute. In this time the shoreward side of San Francisco moved north about fifteen feet, roads were heaved up, water and gas pipes ruptured, buildings fell down, landslides were set in motion, and some buildings simply vibrated themselves into the soft bay muds. Fires started everywhere immediately as short-circuited electricity sparked off escaping gas. Seven hundred people died in a few minutes.

The greatest disasters

The Chinese people don't tell the world many details when disaster strikes their country, so we don't know exactly what happened in the two great earthquakes that have struck China this century. The greatest earthquake that ever struck, however, happened in China in 1556, killing a staggering number of 830,000 people. In 1920, about 180,000 people were killed in China. Then in July, 1976, about 700,000 people lost their lives and the city of T'ang-shan (population 1.6 million) was virtually wiped out.

These disasters were so huge because in certain parts of the country the land is made from loose silty material. It is very fertile and many people farm on it. But when earthquakes happen, the silt flows exactly like water. On these disastrous days in China the hills literally flowed into the valleys where all the people lived, burying them under millions of tons of soil.

The World's Greatest Earthquake Disasters

Date	Country	Numbers Killed (thousands)
856	Greece	45
1290	China	100
1456	Italy	60
1556	China	830
1755	Portugal	60
1847	Japan	34
1908	Italy	160
1920	China	180
1970	Peru	20
1976	Guatemala	23
1976	China	700
1978	Iran	25
1985	Mexico	5
1988	Armenia	25

▼ *Many ancient buildings have been affected by great earthquakes of the past. This temple complex in the Himalayan mountains lies in ruins because of an earthquake. The temple was never reoccupied.*

Emergency

When a disaster hits an area or a country many people will need help. To be effective, those who come to help in an emergency must be clear about what to do. The rescue teams must have prepared a flexible plan.

The scale of the problem

The first thing to do in any emergency is to find out how big the problem is. As soon as an earthquake is over, inspection teams should be air lifted by helicopter to critical places; hospitals, highways, bridges, water mains and aqueducts, dams, and schools. These teams all report back to a central control by radio as soon as possible. At the same time police go by helicopter to take a bird's-eye view of the disaster. They have to find out which places seem in most difficulty, and where the biggest areas of damage are located. They must report back in just the same way as they do for traffic reports every day. The rescue must be kept as much like a normal everyday happening as possible. If emergency teams have been well drilled and they can carry out their tasks without panic, it will be an efficient rescue.

▼ *One of the most important tasks of a rescue team will be to fight fires, especially in buildings where there may still be people trapped. The teams will probably have to carry their own water supplies because the main water pipes are almost certain to have been ruptured by the earthquake.*

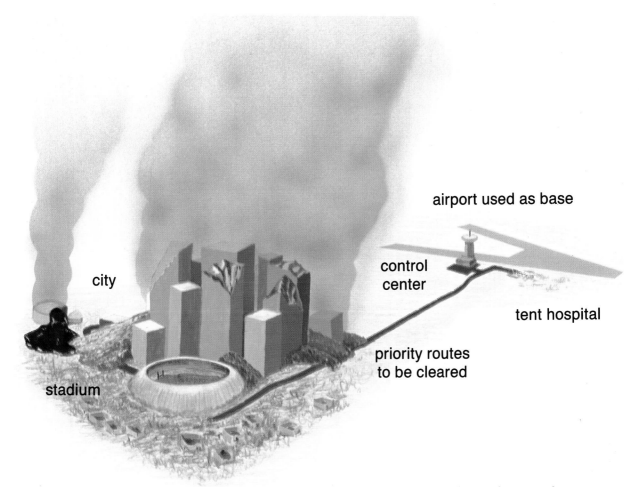

city

stadium

airport used as base

control
center

tent hospital

priority routes
to be cleared

▲   *This diagram shows the way planners
have to organize for the efficient rescue of
people after an earthquake.*

Setting up a control center

Within an hour the size of the disaster will be
known. An airport can be a good place to use
as the control center for the rescue. Even if
the runways are damaged, helicopters can
still land. This means that people can be
taken to other hospitals out of the region. The
massive number of injured people must be
dealt with first. Local hospitals probably
won't be able to cope with so many injured
people even if the hospitals themselves
haven't been damaged. A field hospital made
up of medical tents will have to be set up at
the airport. The huge flat spaces at airports
also have other uses—for storing supplies, for
example.

Coping with broken supply lines

Airport runways can soon be repaired and
supplies can be ferried in by plane. In an
earthquake disaster most of the roads will
be blocked by debris and landslides so that
supply trucks can't get through.

　　As soon as roads are cleared, trucks
will be able to bring in food and water from
distant warehouses along major routes.
These routes must always be cleared first.

　　When earthquakes happen they
usually rupture all the cables and pipes.
There is little water for firefighters to use. In
the 1906 earthquake firemen could only
watch as 28,000 houses burned down
because the water mains were broken.

A plan with feeling

Military efficiency is of great importance in a rescue—but the teams are dealing with people and a sensitive touch is needed. As soon as the earthquake is over people go in search of relatives and friends. Others want to help. Volunteer rescue teams are useful but there must be a plan and someone must be in charge. It is extremely difficult to work both quickly and with feeling.

◄   *This little girl is being rescued from a collapsed building during the early stages of the rescue and before the official teams have arrived on the scene.*

▼   *People need to know who to turn to for help. It is very important for the official rescue team to be easy to recognize. The sign on the rescuers' backs identifies them as members of the Red Cross during the El Salvador earthquake disaster. Notice that much basic life-saving equipment, such as oxygen tanks, will be needed during the emergency period.*

Emergency in Mexico City

When the disaster struck Mexico City in 1985 they had a plan. It didn't work, however, because the scale of the disaster was enormous and there had been no chance to try out the plan. How can anyone practice for a disaster that kills 30,000 people and causes $4 billion damage?

When the disaster happened it had been planned that the military would go on standby and wait for instructions. It was some hours before the size of the disaster was established, and in all this critical time the city officials didn't use the troops.

Mexico is not a rich country. They did not have cranes and bulldozers waiting at special sites just for use in a disaster. It took a number of hours to get the cranes to lift concrete slabs so that rescue teams could get to trapped people. In this time many died. The number of dead was so large the city football stadium was used as a mortuary. No one can really be prepared for an emergency on this scale.

Looking after the homeless

Any earthquake will leave many people homeless. A vital part of the emergency procedure must be to provide shelter for the victims. The first priority will be for blankets. Mexico City, for example, is over 6,500 feet above sea level and even in summer nights can be cold. People who have lost everything need to be fed, and be provided with washing and toilet facilities. Because the drinking water may have been contaminated, the authorities will also have to begin a large-scale vaccination program, or face a major problem of disease.

All of these tasks have to go on without interrupting the rescue of people that remain trapped in the rubble of their homes. It is almost impossible for any one country to cope with so many problems, and it is under these circumstances that outside aid is particularly welcome. It is a time when countries can forget their political differences and help one another.

◄ *Victims of an earthquake huddling under blankets. It is usual for them to be housed in tents as soon as possible.*

Be Prepared

Since an earthquake can strike without warning, leaving thousands dead and hundreds of thousands without homes, how can people be prepared?

Identifying areas at risk

Although small earthquakes occur all over the world, most are too small or too uncommon to worry about. The people who need to be prepared are those living in places of high risk.

To find out how great the risk is, past earthquakes can be plotted on a map. When this was done for the United States, the map showed that most people do not have to be concerned for their safety, because the danger areas are found only on the edges of the country. By examining this map, the government has been able to decide where to concentrate its efforts. Although most countries do not have such good records, scientists can still tell them in general which areas are at greatest risk.

When will the next quake be?

The Earth's plates do not move at an even pace. From time to time the pressure to move is so great that the rocks snap along a line, setting off an earthquake. How long will there be between earthquakes? No one can be certain. Just because there has not been an earthquake for many years does not mean there won't be any more. On the contrary, in fact. Scientists have found that places with many earthquakes have only minor tremors. It is the places with long gaps between quakes that may have the big disasters.

▼ *This map shows where earthquakes occur in the United States. Places with the greatest number of dots have the highest risk.*

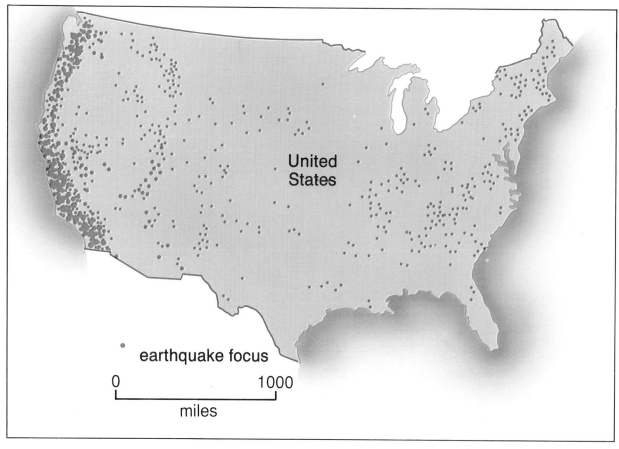

United States

earthquake focus

0   1000

miles

◀ *This device has been used by the Chinese for centuries to predict earthquakes. There is a ball in each of the dragon's heads. When a ball falls into one of the frogs' mouths an earthquake is near. It uses the principle that major earthquakes are often preceded by smaller ones that are hardly noticeable.*

Some scientists have found that the ground starts to swell in the months before an earthquake. People in China also discovered this fact hundreds of years ago. They made their own predicting device (shown above) in which balls fall from a dragon's mouth.

How to design for safety

In an earthquake the ground shakes violently. Buildings collapse or sink into soft materials, landslides occur, and tsunamis are created. People need to be prepared for all these events.

Buildings can be designed so they will not cause disaster. There are inexpensive designs for poor people living in developing countries as well as expensive designs for people living in highly developed areas. No matter what the structure, the rules are the same: design the building to absorb the shock waves, and give it sufficient strength to shake without falling down.

Flexible buildings should be the rule. When the ground vibrates during a tremor, the buildings most likely to collapse are those that are rigid and unbending. Office buildings where the walls and floors are hung from a steel frame will stay up better than those where walls and floors are joined rigidly together. Buildings can also be fitted with "shock absorber" pads of rubber placed between all the joints. When the earthquake comes the rubber padding will help absorb the worst of the shock.

▶ *These long concrete poles are driven through the bay muds in San Francisco to provide good foundations for buildings.*

The most stable kind of building is one that gives just a little with the vibrations. A building that sways violently during a quake can shake itself apart. A square building that can take the force of the vibrations no matter what kind they are is best. This means that buildings with central spaces (called atriums) are not as stable as buildings that are filled in. Oddly shaped buildings are not as stable as those that are regular in shape. Under vibration strangely shaped buildings tend to twist on their foundations.

In a house, the rule is to use materials that will not crack. Buildings made with wooden frames are less likely to fall down than those made of brick and cement. If a roof with wooden tiles collapses, it does not cause as much damage as a roof with heavy slate tiles would. In Iran, for example, the local way of building is to use heavy stones on the roof. In a recent earthquake many people in villages were crushed when their own roofs collapsed.

Above all, the foundations must be good. Many of the buildings that collapsed in Mexico City did so because they rested only on wet peat and mud. This shook like jelly, and so did the buildings situated on it. Foundations must always be taken through to solid rock.

Preparing to stay alive

People in a risk zone have to know how to protect themselves. Unless you can reach a wide open space quickly, running out of a building during a quake might not be a good idea. You could be crushed by falling debris just as you get out of the door.

One of the safer places to be is in the frame of an open door. A door frame will often stand up after the floors have collapsed, because it is one of the strongest parts of a building.

In some buildings of course, such as schools full of students, there simply won't be enough door frames for everyone to shelter under. So in Californian schools, for

▼ *Buildings vibrate during an earthquake. This model gives some idea of the problems that could arise in real life unless architects design them so that they will not crash into one another or split apart.*

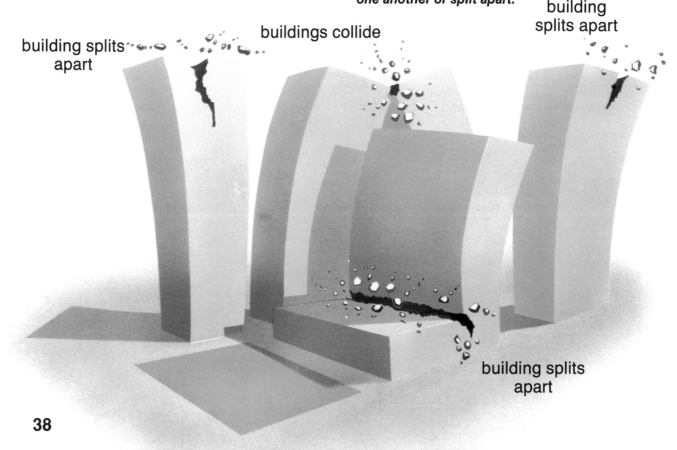

building splits apart

buildings collide

building splits apart

building splits apart

example, the drill is for all students to take cover under their desks. If the ceiling falls the desk will take some of the weight and the chance of being crushed is less.

Tokyo put to the test

In December 1987 the people in Tokyo found out how good their architects and planners were. The earthquake registered 6.6 on the Richter scale. It killed two people and injured 53 out of a city population of ten million. The skyscrapers swayed and rolled as the earthquake gathered intensity and after a minute people in the top floors of the office blocks began to suffer from motion sickness. Nevertheless, every building held firm.

   Computers automatically cut power to hundreds of trains and prepared to stop gas and electricity supplies to reduce the danger of fire. Half of all calls from telephones not specially allocated for use in an emergency were cut off to save the telephone lines from being overloaded. Elevators stopped automatically and stayed off until engineers had checked the safety of the buildings. Although some people were trapped in elevators for up to 90 minutes, all were released unharmed. Tokyo's preparation had worked.

▲　*The design of this skyscraper shows the way the weight of the building is taken through the base. The special design of the supporting struts is to make the structure resist earthquakes.*

◀　*Bridges pose a special design problem. These bridges carrying roads over highways collapsed during California's San Fernando earthquake in 1971. Designers must ensure that this does not happen in the future.*

Waiting for Disaster

California is one of the richest states in the United States. The money earned by its people each year is greater than that of most of the world's countries. If a widespread and large scale disaster happened in this region it would bring much of California's trade to a stop. This would not only be bad for the state, but it would also directly affect the rest of the United States and many overseas countries as well.

Californians know they will have a major earthquake disaster in the next few years. Geological records show that major earthquakes happen very often in California. On average there has been a big earthquake in California every 50 to 100 years.

year	lives lost	cost ($ millions)
1812	40	unknown
1899	6	unknown
1915	6	0.9
1918	0	0.2
1925	13	8.0
1926	1	unknown
1933	115	40.0
1940	9	6.0
1941	0	0.1
1949	0	9.0
1951	0	3.0
1952	14	60.0
1955	0	3.0
1961	0	4.5
1971	65	504.9
1978	0	12.0
1979	0	30.0
1987	6	100.0

▼ **This is what happened to a car when some roofing fell during a recent minor earthquake in the Los Angeles region.**

▲ **This table shows the cost, in human lives and millions of dollars, that the people of Los Angeles have had to bear since they first populated the area heavily.**

Danger for Los Angeles

The table on the facing page shows how many earthquakes have been recorded in southern California, in the region near Los Angeles. In July, 1769, when the first Spanish expedition moved north from Mexico to claim California, they arrived in the Los Angeles region just as four violent earthquakes occurred. So they named the river that flows through Los Angeles "Jesus de los Temblores" which means "Jesus of Our Earthquake" (this is the river now called the Santa Ana). In 1812 there were so many earthquakes that it was called "the year of the earthquakes."

Los Angeles lies directly over an area that is liable to major earthquakes. About 12 million people live in this sprawling urban area. Clearly, when a major earthquake strikes Los Angeles the losses could be very great; if a severe earthquake hit (say about 8.3 on the Richter scale) the city authorities estimate there could be up to 12 thousand deaths, 50 thousand injured, 50 thousand homeless, and damage equal to $25 billion.

Fortunately most of the recent earthquakes in this area have been fairly small and have not caused much loss of life. Although the 1987 earthquake, for example, caused an enormous amount of damage,

▲ *Los Angeles has an almost desert climate and it relies on a network of aqueducts for its water. All of the aqueducts pass over active fault lines. This means that an earthquake which broke the walls of an aqueduct anywhere in southern California could also have disastrous effects on the well-being of the city population.*

only six people were killed. This does not mean that the city authorities are taking no action. There is a team of over 300 scientists and technicians keeping close watch on the region all the time. Moreover, there is a well-rehearsed plan for shutting down nuclear power stations, major pipelines, and lowering the levels of the major reservoirs in the area.

The quake that is overdue

The people of San Francisco are also convinced that the next earthquake will be a large one, although in the surrounding area there has not been a major earthquake for 80 years. San Francisco suffered a terrible earthquake in 1906 giving the first demonstration of how large a disaster can be when an earthquake hits a large, heavily populated city.

► *This is a view of the center of San Francisco. In the foreground are the small hotels and houses on the steep slopes of some hills, and in the background are massive office buildings built on the flat land near the bay.*

To try to minimize the disaster when it comes, the city has insisted on very strict building methods for many years. Government agencies try to keep people aware of the danger. North of the city there is a National Park with a display of earthquake effects. Schools have regular drills so that children know what to do when an earthquake strikes. However, many people have grown tired of the warnings. Few remember the last

earthquake and many think the scientists are just scaremongering about the size of a future disaster. They don't realize that California's time bomb has a very short fuse.

The city built for disaster

Although San Francisco has strict building codes there is much evidence that people still do not take the earthquake threat seriously. Most of San Francisco's homes are built on steep land overlooking the bay. During an earthquake some of the soil on the slopes will slide and carry the houses with it. Near the coast many people have built houses beneath steep slopes. Main roads connecting the city with towns in the south also follow routes beneath steep slopes. Most of the slopes are unstable and landslides are common during heavy rain. An earthquake is certain to shake much soil loose, burying these homes and blocking the main roads. This will not only be disastrous for the people who suffer, but blocked roads may also stop rescue teams from reaching the area quickly.

The city center is built on soft bay muds. These muds are so unstable when shaken by an earthquake that buildings on them will topple over. Here new buildings have deep foundations that reach down to the solid rock beneath. But many of the older buildings have not been brought up to the standards required by new building codes because alterations are very expensive.

Surprisingly, there are also many hospitals and schools built close to the fault line itself. If these large buildings collapse it will be a double disaster. Schools are vital for community shelter and hospitals are essential for treating the injured in an emergency. Schools and hospitals are also normally full of people who are least able to take care of themselves when disaster strikes. When schools and hospitals are allowed to be built in such vulnerable places, it seems that people aren't really convinced that the prediction of a major earthquake is correct.

◄ *These houses are built at the bottom of a steep, unstable slope that might collapse when an earthquake strikes. The landslide that buries the homes would also probably block the main road.*

► *An earthquake will rupture many of the pipes in this major chemical works in San Francisco. There is a risk of both fire and explosion from an accident here.*

Benefits of Earthquakes

While an earthquake occurs it is difficult to imagine that anything good might come of such a disaster. Certainly in the short term this is true. People are killed and injured, many are left shocked and homeless. The most they can hope for at the time is a new house built in a safer way.

We need to take a much longer view to see the benefits. Earthquakes are a sign that the Earth's rocks are splitting, that the Earth is changing shape. Over periods of just tens of years the change can be important. For example, in 1812 there was a terrifying and destructive earthquake in New Madrid, Missouri, which caused the ground to collapse over a large area. However, where the ground had collapsed, it began to fill with water and created a beautiful lake. Reelfoot Lake in western Tennessee is an important tourist spot today, and helps to bring people and money to the area.

Cliffs and rifts

Over millions of years the effects of earthquakes are even more striking. If there is an earthquake in the same place time after time, it often creates a magnificent cliff. In east Africa a huge trench, called a **rift valley,** has been formed by parallel lines of faults. It forms such a distinctive feature that it can be seen from as far away as the moon.

Dramatic valleys

Where an earthquake has happened the rocks are often shattered. The forces of nature can find these places of weak rock and erode them quickly. Old lines of earthquakes (called **fault lines** by scientists) have formed some of the world's most spectacular valleys. Yosemite Valley in California, is a popular tourist area of great beauty. Its deep sided valley has been formed by more than one of nature's forces, but the straight shape shows the fault lines that criss-cross the rocks.

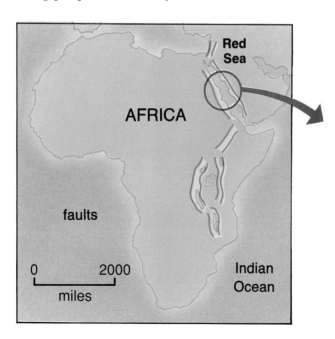

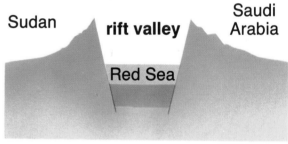

◄ *The world's biggest rift valley makes a scar down the eastern side of Africa, as shown here by yellow shading. It has been formed by two parallel faults. Shock wave after shock wave wracked this area millions of years ago, and the land between the fault lines gradually sank. The rift valley has been partly filled with an arm of the Indian Ocean and now makes the Red Sea. On both sides of the Red Sea there are high mountains, pushed up during the earthquakes.*

▲ *This view of Yosemite Valley is one of the most famous in the world. A glacier has etched out the deep valley, but the valley direction is guided by fault lines. The large peak on the right of the valley is called Half Dome.*

Reservoirs for gas and oil

Many earthquake fault lines still lie buried beneath later rocks and we cannot see them. They often bring benefits even where they are hundreds of feet below the surface. One good example is an **oil trap.** This occurs when rock layers containing oil or gas are pushed against rocks that do not let oil or gas pass. Traps so produced give us much of the oil and gas we use today.

▶ *Oil and gas are often trapped by faults as shown in this diagram.*

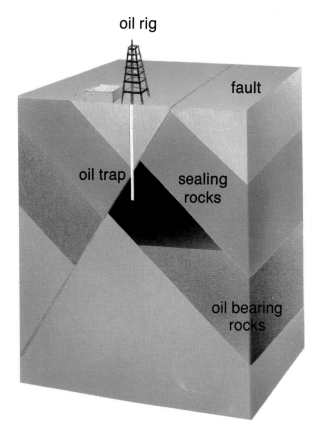

oil rig

fault

oil trap

sealing rocks

oil bearing rocks

Glossary

convection
the circulating movement within a liquid that carries heat from one region to another

core
the inner region of the Earth

crust
the surface layer of the Earth's rock

disaster
a severe event that changes the landscape or disrupts the normal lives of people

earthquake
a violent shaking of the ground surface due to forces within the Earth

fault
the surface that marks the place where two parts of the Earth's crust have slipped past each other. A fault also tells where past earthquakes occurred.

focus
the place within the Earth where an earthquake begins. This is normally tens or even hundreds of miles below the Earth's surface. The snap in the rocks may then extend right to the ground surface.

landslide
a slide of loose rock and soil down a steep slope

mantle
the layer of rock between the Earth's crust and core. The upper part is often liquid.

mudflow
a flow of water and debris that usually looks like brown liquid cement

oil trap
a place where oil becomes trapped below a rock which does not allow oil to pass through it. This is often produced when a fault brings oil-bearing rocks against other rocks.

Pacific Ring of Fire
on the edge of the Pacific Ocean plate there are places where pieces of crust are pushing against one another. This gives rise to many earthquakes, but the edge is also marked by a line of active volcanos and this is where the name "ring of fire" comes from.

A cartoonist's view of the Richter scale

Scale about 5.0

Scale about 6.5

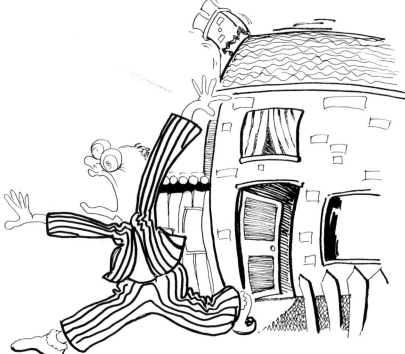
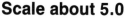

plate

a large part of the Earth's crust that is separated from the rest by large cracks

radioactive substance

a substance such as uranium that gives off heat as its structure changes

reservoir

an artificial lake contained by a dam. It is used to control the amount of water in a river, either to prevent flood or drought.

Richter scale

a scale designed by Charles F. Richter to measure the strength of intensity of shock waves produced by an earthquake. The scale is marked in steps from 1 upward but each increase in 1 unit equals a tenfold increase in the strength of the shock waves. Thus an earthquake that measures 7.0 is 1,000 times more powerful than an earthquake measuring 4.0. Little damage is done by earthquakes below 4.0; an earthquake of 7.0 would cause widespread disaster.

rift valley

a trench in the Earth's surface many miles across and often hundreds of miles long, that has been formed as a strip of land sank between parallel lines of faults

shock waves

the waves of energy that are produced as a rock snaps underground. When they reach the surface the shock waves cause the surface to shake violently. The strength of the shock waves is measured by the Richter scale.

silt

a grade of material slightly finer than sand

tremor

another word to describe the shaking of the ground surface by a set of earthquake shock waves

tsunami

a number of waves of water that are caused by an earthquake or volcanic eruption below an ocean floor. Each wave rushes forward at hurricane speed and arrives on coasts with no warning. So much water is contained in a tsunami that the waves flood up to one mile inland. A tsunami wave may be 15-50 feet high.

Scale about 8.0

Index

Africa 44
Alaska 20, 21, 27, 28
Alps 17
Anchorage 28
Andes 14-16

California 21, 24, 25, 27, 38, 39, 40-43, 44
China 17, 28, 30, 31, 37
convection 4, 5, 46
core 4, 46
Crescent City, Calif. 27
crust 4, 46

dams 17, 22, 23, 24
disaster 4, 46

Earth 4
earthquake (definition) 46
earthquake control 24-25
emergency measures 32-35

faults 7, 8, 24, 25, 44, 45, 46
focus 6, 7, 8, 9, 27, 46

Greece 31
Guatemala 26, 31

Hawaii 21
Hoover Dam 22, 23
Huascaran 14, 15

India 24
Iran 31, 38
Italy 17, 31

Japan 21, 31, 39

Koyna Dam 24

landslide 14, 17, 27, 46
Los Angeles 25, 40-41

man-made earthquakes 22-25
mantle 4, 46
Mexico 31, 35
Mexico City 6, 8-13, 35, 38
mudflow 14, 15, 16, 46

New Madrid, Mo. 6, 29, 44

oil trap 45, 46

Pacific Ocean 18, 20, 21
Pacific Ring of Fire 20, 46
Pemex Tower 9, 10
Peru 14, 31
plate 4, 6, 47
Portugal 21, 31
prediction 36-37

radioactive 4, 47
Red Sea 44
reservoir 23, 24, 47
Richter scale 23, 24, 29-30, 4l, 46-67
rift valley 44, 47
risk 6, 22, 36, 38

San Francisco 25, 27, 29, 30, 42-43
shock waves 6, 7, 8, 14, 37, 47
silt 17, 30, 47

T'ang-shan 17, 31
Tokyo 39
tremor 8, 11, 17, 37, 47
tsunami 7, 18-21, 27,47

United States 6, 22, 27, 28, 29, 30, 36, 40-42, 44, 45

Vaiont 17

Yosemite 45
Yungay 14-17